Sky Pig

by Jan L. Coates

Illustrated by Suzanne Del Rizzo

pajamapress

First published in Canada and the United States in 2016

Text copyright © 2016 Jan L. Coates
Illustration copyright © 2016 Suzanne Del Rizzo
This edition copyright © 2016 Pajama Press Inc.
This is a first edition.

10 9 8 7 6 5 4 3 2 1

www.pajamapress.ca   info@pajamapress.ca

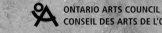

The publisher gratefully acknowledges the support of the Canada Council for the Arts and the Ontario Arts Council for its publishing program. We acknowledge the financial support of the Government of Canada through the Canada Book Fund (CBF) for our publishing activities.

Library and Archives Canada Cataloguing in Publication

Coates, Jan L., 1960-, author
    Sky pig / by Jan L. Coates ; illustrated by Suzanne Del Rizzo.
ISBN 978-1-927485-98-9 (bound)

    I. Del Rizzo, Suzanne, illustrator II. Title.
PS8605.O238S59 2016   jC813'.6   C2015-906434-1

Publisher Cataloging-in-Publication Data (U.S.)

Coates, Jan, 1960-
  Sky Pig / by Jan L. Coates ; illustrated by Suzanne Del Rizzo.
  [32] pages : color illustrations ; cm.
Summary: "Ollie the pig dreams of flight, and enlists his human friend Jack to help him build wings, kites, and other clever contraptions to reach the sky" – Provided by publisher.
ISBN-13: 978-1-927485-98-9
1. Pigs -- Juvenile fiction. 3. Flight – Juvenile fiction. 3. Children and animals – Juvenile fiction. I. Title. II. Del Rizzo, Suzanne.
[E] dc23 PZ7.C638Sk 2016

Cover and book design—Rebecca Bender
Manufactured by by Sheck Wah Tong Printing Ltd.
Printed in Printed in Hong Kong, China

Pajama Press Inc.
181 Carlaw Ave. Suite 207 Toronto, Ontario Canada, M4M 2S1

Distributed in Canada by UTP Distribution
5201 Dufferin Street Toronto, Ontario Canada, M3H 5T8

Distributed in the U.S. by Ingram Publisher Services
1 Ingram Blvd. La Vergne, TN 37086, USA

The illustrations were rendered with plasticine, polymer clay, paper collage, milkweed fluff, watch gears, and other doodads

For my parents, and for determined dreamers everywhere —J.L.C.

To Sharon, my aunt, for inspiring and nurturing my creative spirit since I was little —S.D.

One blustery day, Ollie stood on his tippy toes, waving his trotters at the sky. He smiled up at birds and bugs, airplanes, dandelion fluff, and leaves.

"Really?" Jack asked. Ollie nodded.

Together, Ollie and Jack began collecting leafy branches.
Ollie tried not to wiggle as his friend fastened them onto his back.

Ollie looked up, way up, at the leaves
swirling above the windy hill.
"Let's go," Jack said.

Together, they climbed and climbed to the very top of the very high hill.

"Run, Ollie, run!" Jack shouted.
And Ollie did run — as fast as ever a pig could run.

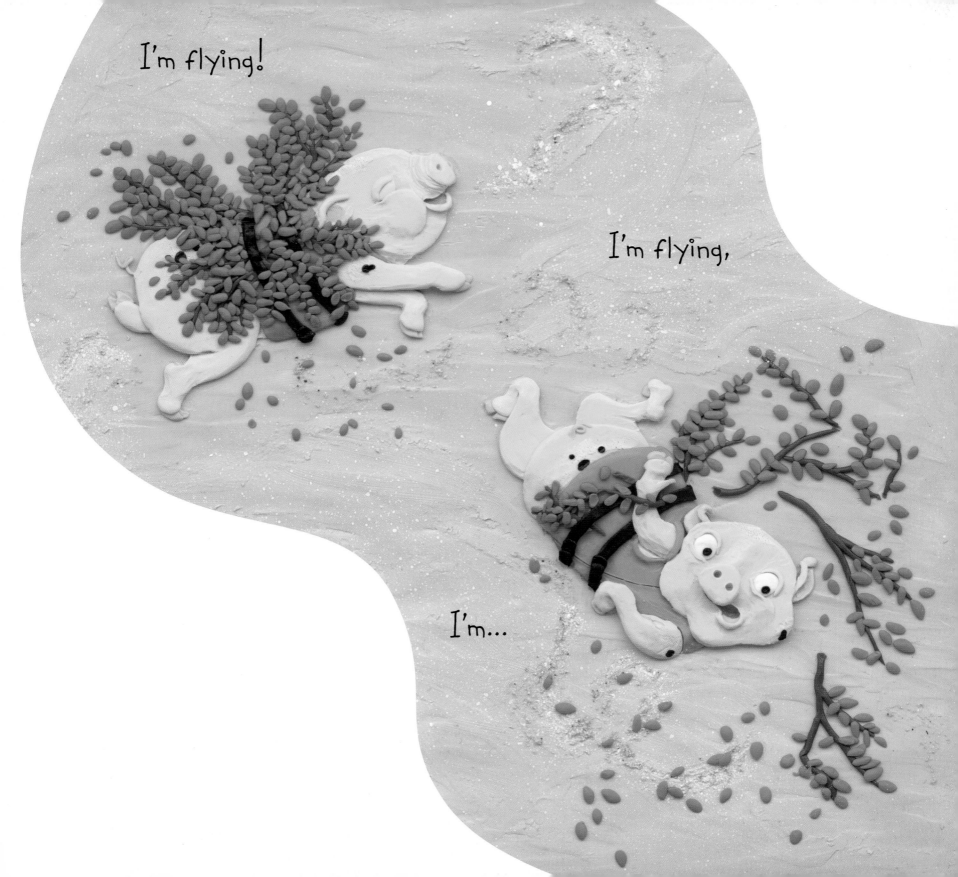

"Oink! Oink!"
"Whoa! Are you okay, Ollie?"
Ollie shook his head, then hobbled home to his sandbox.

The very next day he spotted two kites, dipping
and swooping like dancers.

Garden stakes, twine, and a feed sack—Ollie dropped them into Jack's lap, then pointed his snout at the kites.

"Really?" Jack asked. Ollie nodded.

He stood still while Jack hooked the kite string to his collar.
Together they climbed and climbed to the very top of the very high hill.

Jack tossed the kite up into the air, then Ollie raced down the hill. A strong breeze caught the kite at once.

I'm flying!

I'm flying,

I'm...

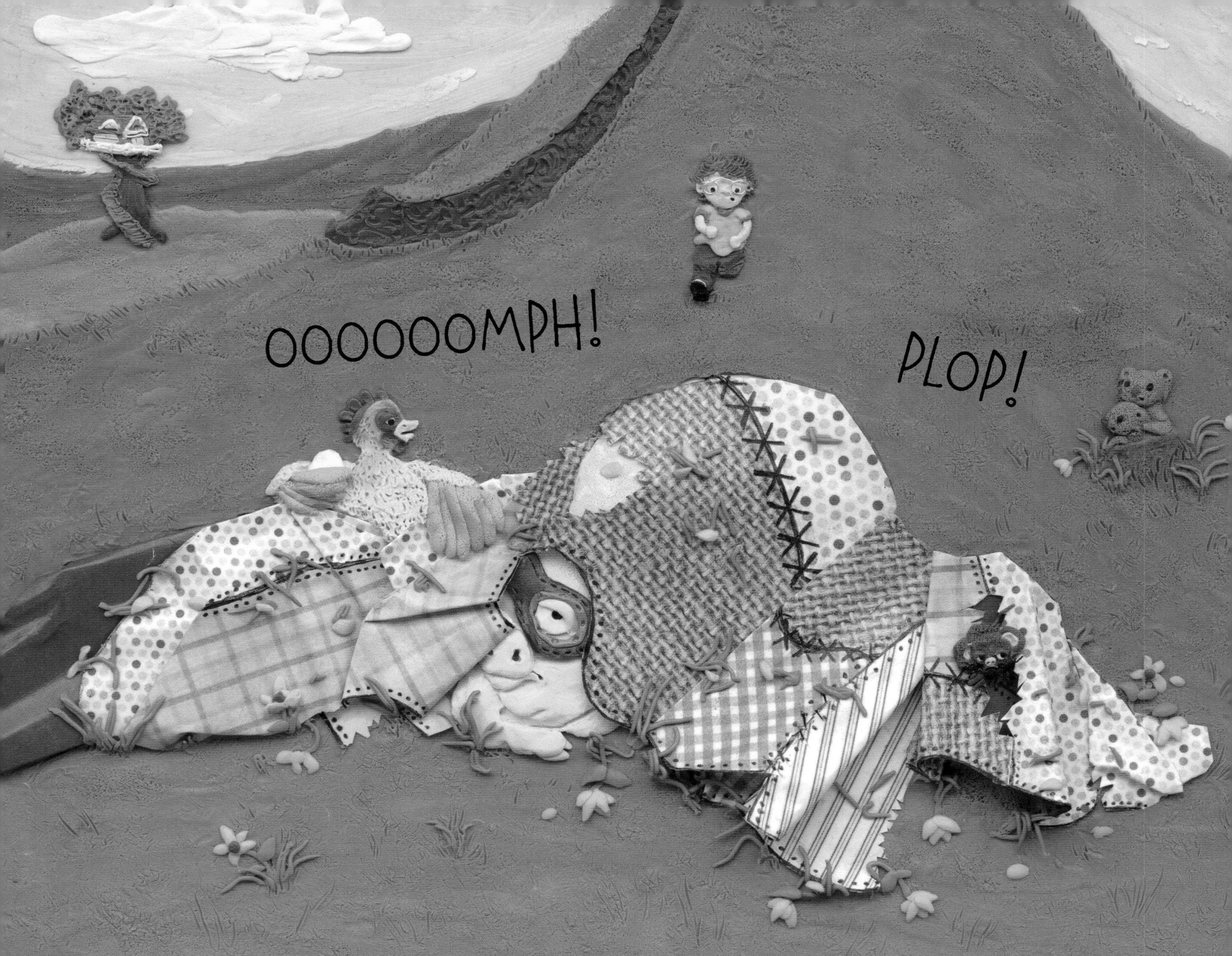

"Oink! Oink!"
"Oh, no! Are you okay, Ollie?"

Ollie stopped rolling, then limped home to wallow in his mud hole.

A gaggle of honking geese passed overhead; Ollie looked at Jack. Then he looked from the chicken coop to the duck pond to the bird feeders.

"Really?" Jack said.

Ollie nodded.

Jack sighed.

Chicken
Duck pond

Ollie's ears twitched as Jack fastened the tickly wings to his back.

"Just like an eagle," Jack said, flapping his arms. "Are you ready?"

Ollie trotted over to the wagon.
The two friends climbed and climbed to
the very top of the very high hill.

Jack ran, pulling the
wagon behind him. Ollie
closed his eyes as the
wind ruffled his wings.
Suddenly, the rumbling
of the wagon beneath
him disappeared.

I'm flying!

I'm flying,

I'm...

Ollie groaned as Jack helped him into the wagon and took him home to a warm bubble bath.

Ollie continued sky-gazing, as sadly as ever a deeply-disappointed pig could gaze. Belly rubs, apples, mud frolics—nothing made him smile.

One lazy morning, raindrops splattered against the windows. But what was that? Ollie peered out at an umbrella somersaulting then soaring out of sight.

He found the umbrella in a cornfield and carried it back to the barn.

"Really? Like Mary Poppins?" said Jack. "You'll need more than one."

Ollie wagged his tail and bounced along the path up to the very top of the very high hill. Jack dragged behind.

When they got to the top, the umbrellas flapped and fluttered. Ollie took off, rolling downhill as fast as ever a pig could roll.

I'm flying!

I'm flying,

I'm...

OOOOOOMPH! PLOP!

"Oink! Oink!"
"Oh, no! Are you okay, Ollie?"
Jack folded up the umbrellas and
helped his friend wobble home.
"I'm sorry, Ollie," he said.

At bedtime, Ollie shuffled outside and stood perfectly still, staring up at a million twinkling stars.

The next day, Ollie flumped down in the sunshine and sighed. A giant shadow made him look up, way up. He smiled. Then he climbed and climbed to the very top of the very high hill.

Ollie didn't hesitate. He scrambled up into the basket, then stood on his tippy toes, peeking out over the side.

"You're flying!" Jack yelled. "You're flying. Ollie, you ARE flying!"

And Ollie looked down at his friend and grinned, as much as ever a flying pig could grin.

Balloon Rides $5